Visiting Day

Dr. Lena Johnson

PAGE PUBLISHING
Conneaut Lake, PA

First originally published by Page Publishing 2022

ISBN 978-1-6624-8844-3 (pbk)
ISBN 978-1-6624-8843-6 (digital)

Printed in the United States of America

Dedicated to my daughter Morgan, who always remembers to go visit the ones she loves, near or far.

Today is the day!
It's time to get up!
Get out of bed and
Get dressed, sleepy head!

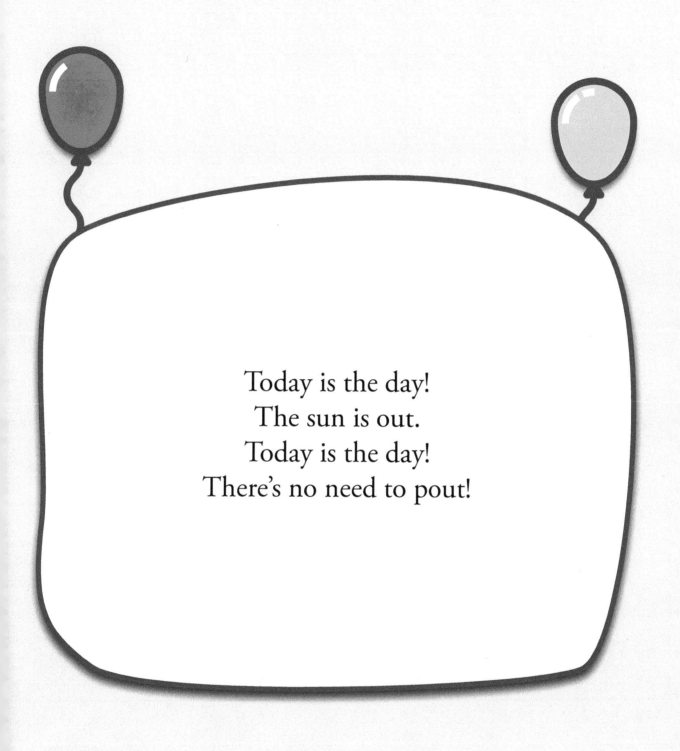

Today is the day!
The sun is out.
Today is the day!
There's no need to pout!

Today is the day!
We're off on our way.
The car ride is long,
So let's sing a song!

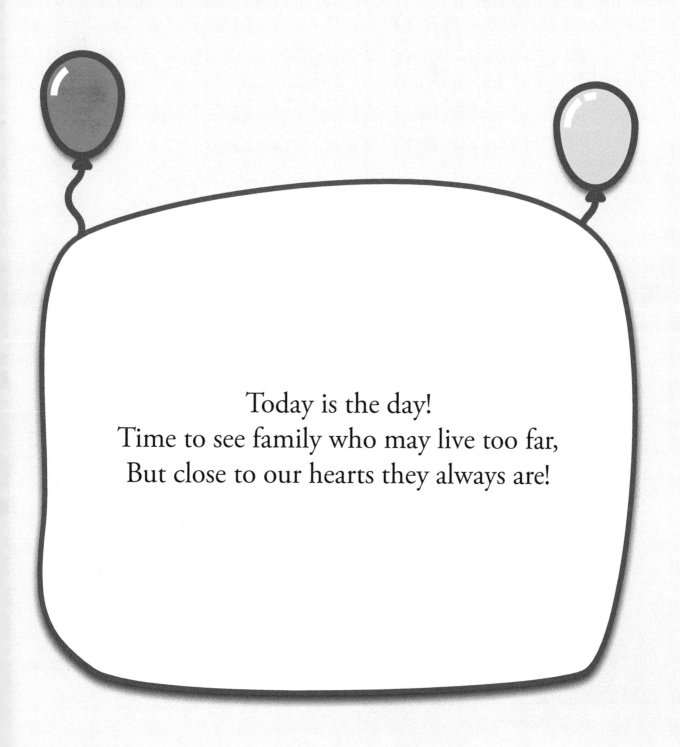

Today is the day!
Time to see family who may live too far,
But close to our hearts they always are!

Today is the day!
Hip, hip, hooray!
When family and friends come together
No matter what the weather!

Today is the day!
Laughing and playing,
Hugging and praying. Hip, hip, hooray!
It's visiting day!

Today was the day!
Now it's time to go.
We had lots of fun,
And we will miss you so!

Today was the day!
Now the day is done.
Thank you for coming.
We had lots of fun!

Today was the day!
Thank you for staying.
Thank you for playing.
Until we meet again.
Until the next
visiting day.

Afterword

Whether incarcerated, in a nursing home, or in a care facility and whether living near or far, it is important to take the time to call, write, or visit your friends, family, and loved ones. Building and maintaining relationships takes time, effort, and work—work that is necessary to living, learning, coping, laughing, and growing. What you may view as a half hour of boring dad stories may be the highlight of their day, week, or year. Time is precious. Family and friends even more so. Cherish the time you have however short it may be.

About the Author

Lena Johnson was born and raised in Bremerton in the beautiful evergreen state of Washington. Lena has three amazing kids and an amazing husband, each contributing to her book ideas. Lena's inspiration for this book comes from her daughter Morgan, who always takes time to remember the friends and family who are important to her. Spending time with her family and friends is always cherished. When Lena isn't spending time with her friends and family, you can almost always find her sitting on her deck, drinking coffee with her pudgy black pug, Sumo.

CPSIA information can be obtained
at www.ICGtesting.com
Printed in the USA
LVHW070746290322
714644LV00006B/45

9 781662 488443